E
Del   Del Negro, Janice.
           Willa and the wind

Willa and the Wind

For my sister, Joan (and for Willa, of course)
— J. M. D.

To George
— H. S.

Marshall Cavendish • New York London Singapore • Text copyright © 2005 by Janice M. Del Negro • Illustrations copyright © 2005 by Heather Solomon
All rights reserved • Marshall Cavendish, 99 White Plains Road, Tarrytown, NY 10591 • www.marshallcavendish.us • Library of Congress Cataloging-in-Publication Data • Willa and the wind / retold by Janice M. Del Negro; illustrated by Heather Solomon. • p. cm. • Summary: A mischievous north wind and a dishonest innkeeper try to outsmart young Willa Rose Mariah McVale, who must use trickery to claim what is rightfully hers. • ISBN 0-7614-5232-X [1. Winds—Fiction. 2. Barter—Fiction. 3. Farm life—Fiction. 4. Taverns (Inns)—Fiction.] I. Solomon, Heather, ill. II. Title. • PZ7.D38314Wi 2005 [E]—dc22 • 2004025715 • The text of this book is set in Adobe Garamond. • The illustrations are rendered in watercolor, collage, acrylic, and oils. • Printed in China • First edition • 1 3 5 6 4 2

Marshall Cavendish
Children

Willa and the Wind

retold by Janice M. Del Negro   illustrated by Heather Solomon

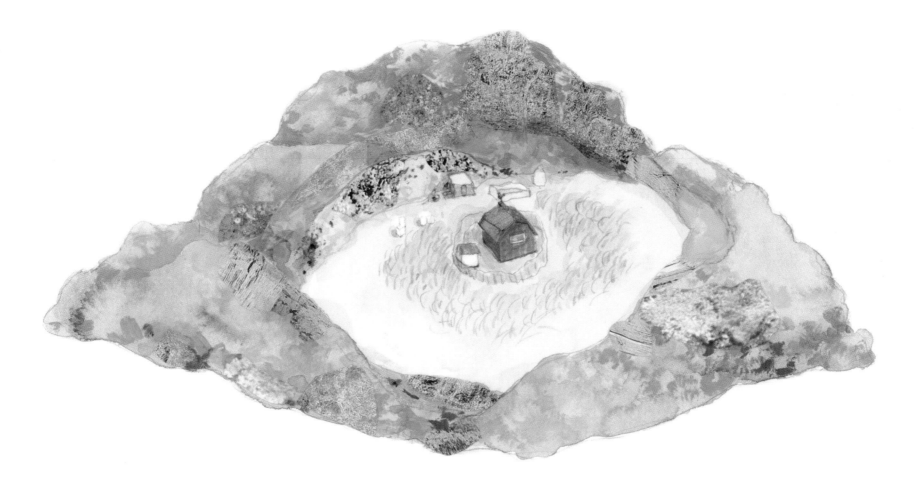

Marshall Cavendish Children

Author's note

Willa and the Wind is an original story based on "The Lad Who Went to the North Wind, " a Norwegian folktale found in Peter Asbjørnsen and Jørgen Moe's *Popular Tales from the Norse* (2nd ed., E.P. Dutton, 1907).

—J. M. D.

Willa was born in a windy valley in the windy
middle of nowhere. She lived in a small house on a small
farm with her big sister, and as long as the wind blew and the
clouds rained, the two sisters always had enough.

But one summer the wind took a holiday. The sun scorched the cornfields dry, and it burned the girls' noses red.

"Willa," called Sis. "Go out to the barn and fetch some cornmeal so we can have corn bread and honey for breakfast."

"It's too hot to cook," Willa grumbled, but off she went. As Willa made her way back to the kitchen, the north wind swooped down out of the mountains. He was on holiday from work, but not from making mischief. WHOOSH! He blew birds, leaves, and Willa across the barnyard. WHOOSH! He blew the last bit of cornmeal right out of the bowl. And WHOOSH! He flew off hooting in a cloud of yellow dust.

"You ornery sack of no-good wind!" Willa shouted. "You bring that cornmeal back!"

"Well, don't have a hissy," said Sis. "If you want cornbread that badly, go get it."

"I'm going, I'm going." Willa stomped down the road, bound for the mountains and the home of Old Windy, the north wind.

Old Windy lived in a great stone house on the side of a great stone mountain. Anyone else would have been afraid, but Willa marched up the stone steps to that front door and pounded on it. Old Windy himself whistled down from the top of the house, blew open the door with a great blast, and roared . . .

"Don't yell at me, you no-good, no-account thieving windbag. I am Willa Rose Mariah McVale, and I want the cornmeal you stole, so give it back!"

Old Windy huffed and puffed, started and stopped, and finally spluttered, "**GO AWAY!**" Then he slammed the door.

"Humph," said Willa, and she pounded on the door again.

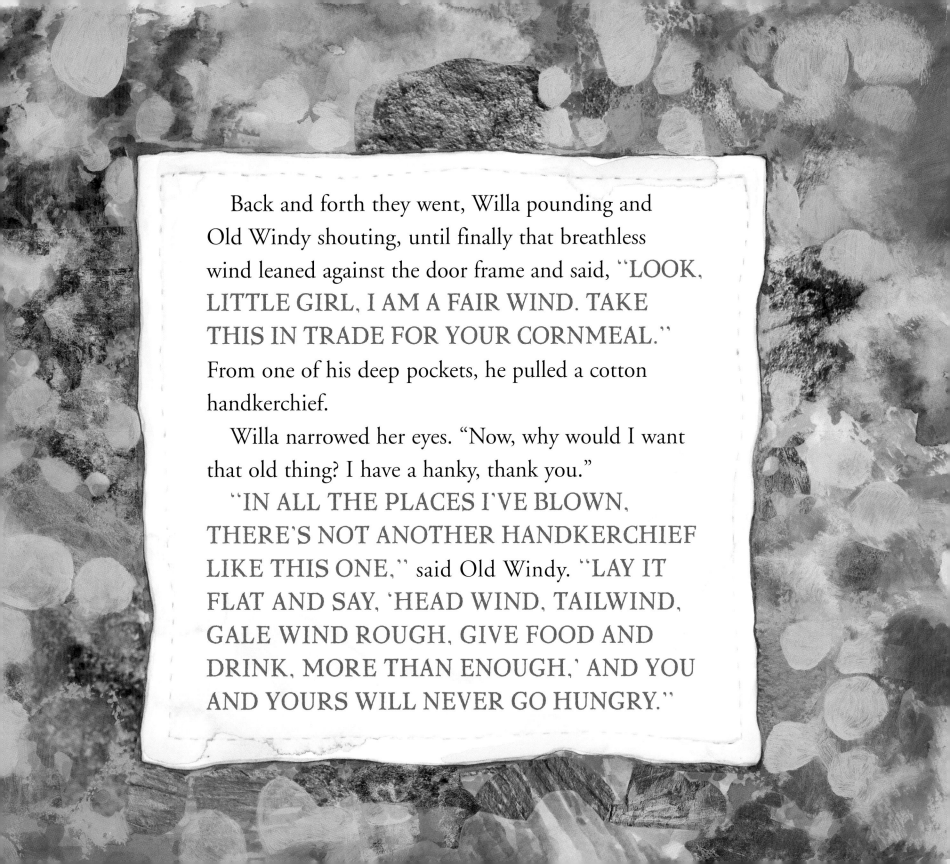

Back and forth they went, Willa pounding and Old Windy shouting, until finally that breathless wind leaned against the door frame and said, "LOOK, LITTLE GIRL, I AM A FAIR WIND. TAKE THIS IN TRADE FOR YOUR CORNMEAL." From one of his deep pockets, he pulled a cotton handkerchief.

Willa narrowed her eyes. "Now, why would I want that old thing? I have a hanky, thank you."

"IN ALL THE PLACES I'VE BLOWN, THERE'S NOT ANOTHER HANDKERCHIEF LIKE THIS ONE," said Old Windy. "LAY IT FLAT AND SAY, 'HEAD WIND, TAILWIND, GALE WIND ROUGH, GIVE FOOD AND DRINK, MORE THAN ENOUGH,' AND YOU AND YOURS WILL NEVER GO HUNGRY."

Willa tucked the hanky in her apron pocket and started home. The sun set behind the trees, and Willa knew it would be dark before she reached the safety of her sister's kitchen. She saw an inn by the side of the road, and she knocked on the door.

"Please, sire," Willa asked the innkeeper. "May I sleep by your fire tonight?"

"Well, girl, the fire burns with or without you in front of it," he said.

Willa went in and settled by the hearth. Then she unfolded the wind's handkerchief and whispered, "Head wind, tailwind, gale wind rough, give food and drink, more than enough." Sure as the wind blows, the hanky was spread with the finest food and drink, and Willa sat and ate her fill.

When the innkeeper heard the
words and saw the magical feast,
his heart turned moldy with greed.
That night, while Willa slept, the
innkeeper crept to where she lay and
gently, gently pulled the wind's
hanky from her pocket and left
one of his own in its place.
Willa woke in the morning
none the wiser, and, handkerchief
in her pocket, she hurried
home. Sis was tending
the bees.

"Welcome home," she said.
"Where's the cornmeal?"

"I have something better than cornmeal," said Willa, and she spread
the handkerchief on the ground and chanted the magic words.

Nothing happened.

"It's a handkerchief," said Sis.
Willa thought about having a fit
and falling in it, but instead she
marched off to pay a second visit
to Old Windy.
Old Windy's great stone house loomed
above her. Willa went up to the door and
pounded on it. Old Windy came whistling
down the stone stairs, flung open the
stone door, and howled, "WHO ARE
YOU AND WHAT DO YOU WANT?"

"You know very well who I am. I want that cornmeal you stole because that hanky you gave me isn't worth a spoon of spit."

``I'D THANK YOU TO REMEMBER THAT I AM AN HONEST WIND. HERE. TAKE THIS AND GO AWAY.``

Reaching behind him, he drew forth . . .

. . . a billy goat.

Willa looked at the goat. She looked at Old Windy.

"Why, exactly, do I want this goat? He'll eat everything he's not supposed to, he doesn't give milk, and he smells like a goat."

"IN ALL THE PLACES I'VE BLOWN, THERE'S NOT ANOTHER GOAT LIKE THIS ONE. TICKLE THE GOAT AND SAY THE WORDS 'HEAD WIND, TAILWIND, GALE WIND BOLD, FILL EMPTY POCKETS FULL OF GOLD,' AND FROM HIS MOUTH THIS GOAT WILL DROP ENOUGH GOLD COINS TO FILL YOUR TWO CUPPED HANDS."

Willa thanked the north wind for the goat and started home. Darkness fell, and once again she turned off the road to the inn.

"Well, girl," the innkeeper said, "you may have a place by the fire, for that burns with or without you, but the goat will have to go to the barn."

Willa led the goat to the barn, but before she left, she tickled him under his chin and whispered Old Windy's words, and sure as the wind blows, that goat opened his mouth and dropped enough coins to fill Willa's two cupped hands. She returned to the inn, where she paid for a fine supper and a fine night's rest.

She would not have slept so soundly had she known the innkeeper had seen her with the wondrous goat and wanted it for his own. So, in the middle of the night, the innkeeper took Willa's goat and left one that looked exactly like it in his place.

In the morning, Willa was none the wiser. She took the animal by its tether and led it home.

Sis was feeding the chickens. She took one whiff and held her nose.

"Willa, wherever you got it, you can't keep it!"

"Oh, we'll keep it, all right." Willa laughed. "Watch! Head wind, tailwind, gale wind bold, fill empty pockets full of gold."

But sure as the wind blows, what that goat dropped had nothing to do with gold.

Willa left Sis spreading fertilizer in the garden and tore back to Old Windy's. She went up to the great front door and pounded on it. Old Windy came whistling down from the top of the house, threw open the door, and blasted,

"WHO ARE YOU AND . . .
OH, IT'S YOU."

Willa looked at him sternly.

"Now, I don't know what kind of sneaky windblown shenanigans you're up to, but that hanky you gave me isn't worth a spoon of spit and that goat you gave me isn't worth a bag of bees. Besides, they only worked once, and what kind of trade is that?"

Old Windy didn't even blink. He reached into his deep sleeve and pulled out a wooden whistle.

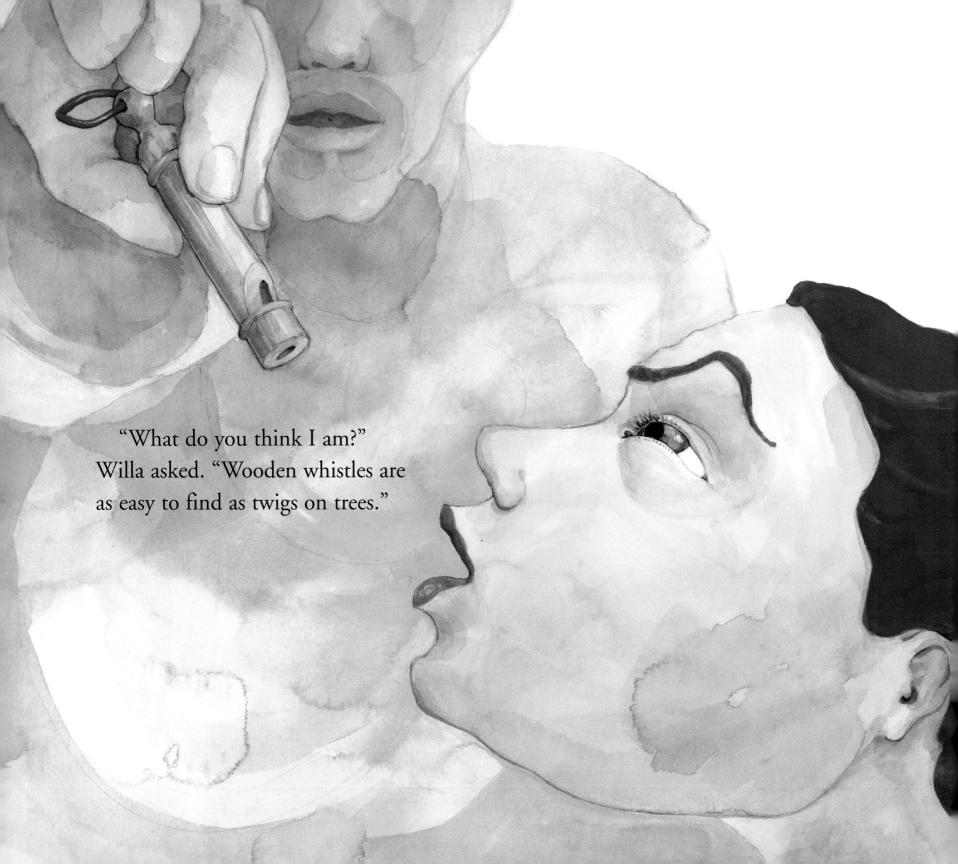

"What do you think I am?"
Willa asked. "Wooden whistles are
as easy to find as twigs on trees."

"IN ALL THE PLACES I'VE BLOWN, THERE'S NOT ANOTHER WHISTLE LIKE THIS ONE," the north wind said. "ALL YOU NEED TO SAY IS, 'HEAD WIND, TAILWIND, GALE WIND SPIN, TWIRL THEM, SPIN THEM WITHOUT END.'"

"Then what?" asked Willa.

"THEN BLOW THE WHISTLE. YOU WILL WHISTLE UP A WHIRL OF A WIND THAT WILL SPIN WHOMEVER, WHATEVER, WHICHEVER AROUND UNTIL YOU WHISTLE IT DOWN."

He handed her the whistle.

"ON YOUR WALK HOME TONIGHT, CONSIDER THAT I AM AN HONORABLE WIND."

Willa pocketed the whistle and started home. A wisp of an idea blew her mind clear, and she headed straight to the inn.

"Well, girl!" the innkeeper said. "Have you come for another fine meal?"

Willa sighed. "Alas, I have no money. I have come only to beg a place by your fire."

Eyeing the wooden whistle peeking from her pocket, the innkeeper said, "The fire burns whether you are in front of it or not."

That night, Willa lay down by the fire, the whistle in her pocket, and it wasn't long before she breathed the deep, loud sighs of sleep.

Now, the innkeeper hadn't seen Willa do anything with the whistle, but he was certain that if the hanky was magic, and the goat was magic, then the whistle was magic, too. In the light of the windy dawn, he crept to where Willa slept. Gently, gently, out of her pocket, he stole the wooden whistle.

He ran outside and blew on it. Nothing.

He blew again. Nothing.

He blew himself blue. Still nothing.

He threw the whistle down and stamped his feet.

Willa, watching from the door, whisked out of the inn, scooped up the whistle, chanted the magic words, and blew.

The whistle sounded sweet and clear.

A small breeze tickled the back of the innkeeper's neck. The breeze circled from inn to barn and back again. A wisp of wind whirled the magic handkerchief out of the innkeeper's pocket. A tiny tornado twirled the goat out of the barn. A huff of hurricane swirled the innkeeper around and around until . . .

"Mercy!" he cried. "Mercy!"

"You don't deserve it," Willa said with a sniff.

She tucked the handkerchief into her pocket and took the goat by his tether. Then, and only then, did she blow on the wooden whistle and whistle down the wind.

"Behave yourself from now on," said Willa, "or I'll come back and whistle you dizzy."

Sis was frowning at the dusty garden when Willa stepped into the yard, whispered the words, and blew on her whistle. The wind picked up, gray clouds spun across the hot blue sky, and the rain began to fall.

"Willa, you brought the wind—and the rain!" Sis laughed.

"And that's not all," said Willa.

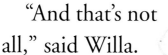

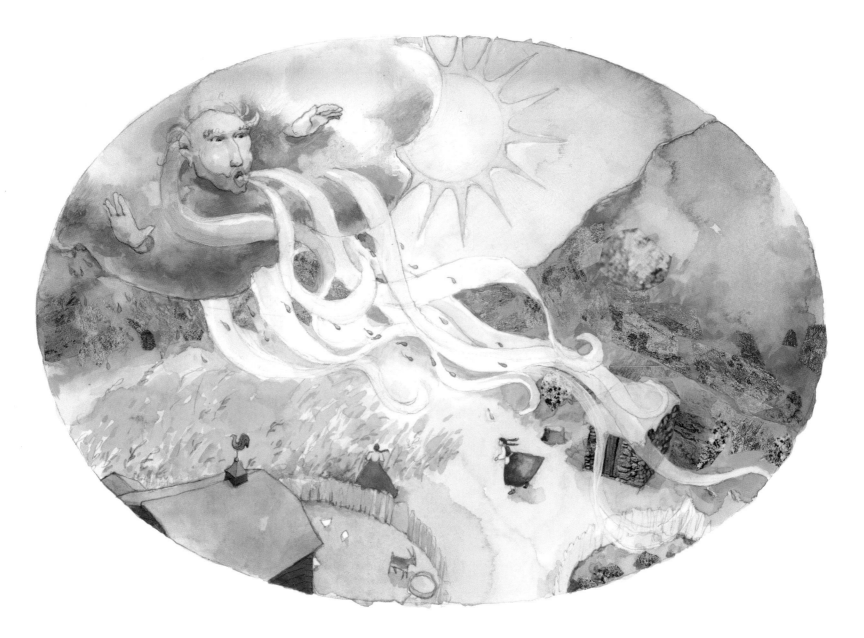

Ever since then, in that windy valley in the windy middle
of nowhere, even in the driest summers in the hottest years,
the wind whistles softly, and the rain falls cool and sweet.